To: Miss "Long Legs"
Merry Christmas
From:
Miss Annette.
I ♥ U.
2019

A TALE FROM
THE LAND OF STORIES

Trollbella Throws a Party

By **Chris Colfer**

Illustrated by **Brandon Dorman**

LITTLE, BROWN AND COMPANY
NEW YORK BOSTON

Once upon a time, there was a little troll girl named Trollbella. She was the queen of an underground kingdom where trolls and goblins lived. Trollbella's favorite thing about being queen was getting to throw big birthday parties for herself, and this year she wanted her party to be extra special.

So the little troll queen ordered a cake that was so tall she needed a ladder to blow out the candles. She got herself stacks of presents that piled all the way up to the kingdom's rocky ceiling.

"I have forty layers of cake and presents
by the dozen, but this party feels incomplete,"
Trollbella said. "Something is missing, but
I don't know what."

So Trollbella added a clown, who made her balloons, and a magician, who did incredible tricks. She had a face painter, who gave her whiskers and stripes like a tiger. She hired a band of goblin musicians, who played all her favorite tunes.

"I thought jokes, magic, and music would make my party a blast," Trollbella said. "Every troll queen deserves to have fun on her birthday, but I'm as bored as a sunken ship!"

To make her party an even bigger thrill, Trollbella brought in a petting zoo of magical creatures! There were unicorns, griffins, mermaids, and baby dragons! There were two-headed puppies and a litter of rainbow kittens!

"The animals are fuzzy, slippery, scaly, and cute, but this party is hardly a hoot," Trollbella said. "I never thought I'd ask this, but: Have I gotten too old for birthday parties? Is that even possible?"

In her last attempt to make the party a hit, Trollbella threw herself a carnival. There was a Ferris wheel, a carousel, and a roller coaster! There were swings and slides and bounce houses! It was everything a troll girl could want!

Unfortunately, it still wasn't enough to make the troll queen happy. Looking at all the exciting things around her only made Trollbella feel empty.

Just then, Trollbella heard a great big laugh come from the Ferris wheel.

"I didn't give anyone permission to have fun," she said. "How dare they enjoy my party without me?"

Trollbella found a tiny goblin boy who had snuck into her party. He smiled and squealed as the Ferris wheel looped around. He was having so much fun that Trollbella grinned and giggled just from watching him.

When the Ferris wheel came to a stop, the goblin
boy saw Trollbella and shivered in fear.

"Your Trollness, please forgive me!" the goblin boy said. "I didn't mean to be rude. You see, it's my birthday, too, but my family is poor, so I didn't get very much. Your party looked like so much fun, I couldn't resist it!"

Nothing at the party was making her happy except seeing the goblin boy smile. Suddenly, Trollbella understood what her party had been missing, and she knew how to fix it.

"Are you kidding?" she told the goblin boy. "This party is all for *you*!
You've just ruined the surprise! Now go get your friends and family!
Tell the whole kingdom to come join your celebration!"

The goblin boy couldn't believe his ears. No one had ever done anything so nice for him in his whole life! He raced through all the troll and goblin neighborhoods, spreading the word, and returned with everyone in the kingdom.

"Welcome, ghoulish subjects!" Trollbella said. "It's this goblin boy's birthday, and I order you to have some fun! So grab some cake and take home some presents! Let's make this party one we'll all remember!"

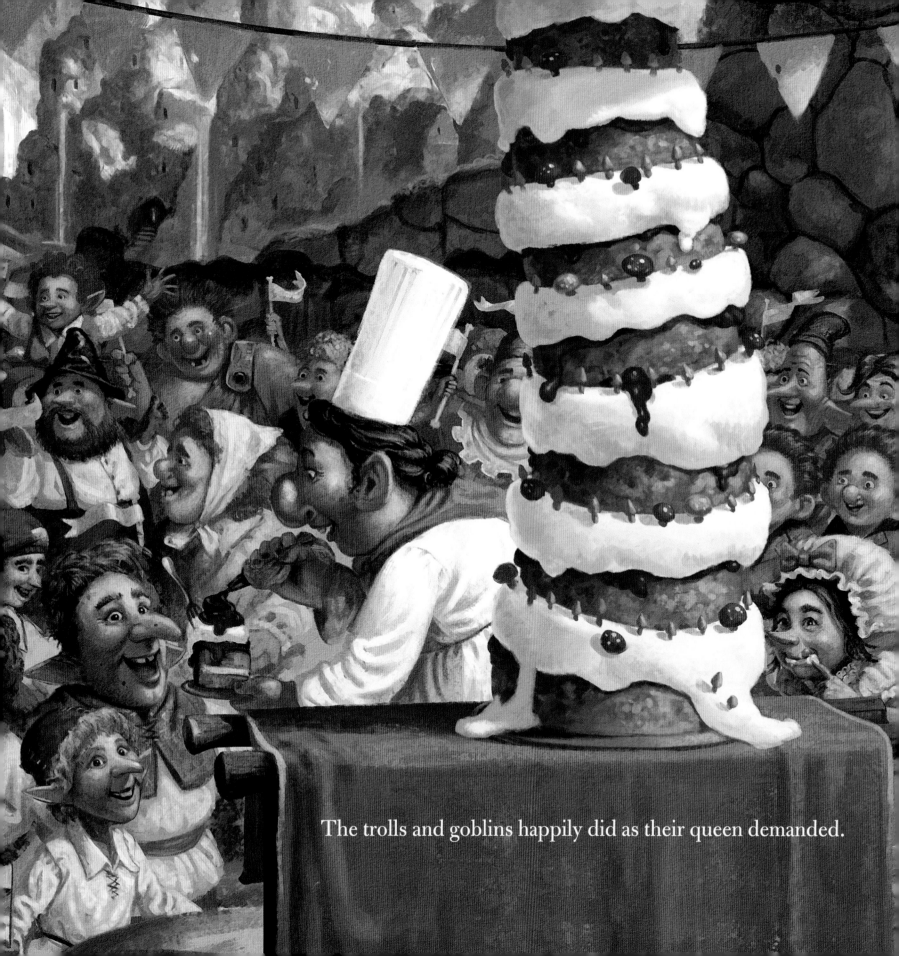

The trolls and goblins happily did as their queen demanded.

They laughed at the clown and were dazzled by the magician.

They danced to the music until their feet started to ache, then they had their faces painted. They petted all the animals in the magical zoo, then rode all the rides in the carnival until their stomachs couldn't take any more.

The goblin boy's excitement grew as he watched all his friends and family have such a good time! However, when the party was over, his smile started to fade.

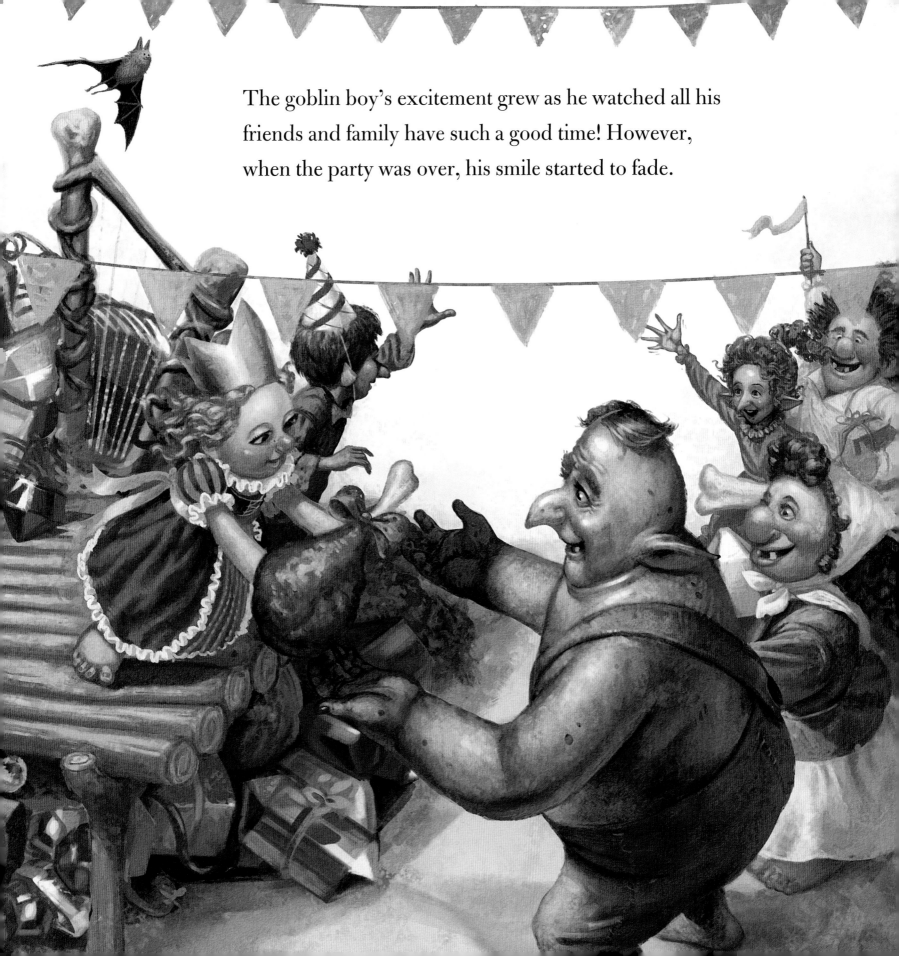

"What's wrong?" Trollbella asked. "Does the splendor and awesomeness of your party overwhelm you?"

"No, the party is wonderful, like something from a dream!" he said.
"But it's your birthday, too, and I have nothing to give *you*."

"Don't be silly, little goblin boy," Trollbella said. "Seeing you smile was the best present a troll girl could ask for. Everything is much more fun when you have someone to share it with."

ABOUT THIS BOOK

This book was edited by Alvina Ling and Bethany Strout
and designed by Kristina Iulo under the art direction of Saho Fujii.
The production was supervised by Erika Schwartz, and the production editor
was Andy Ball. The illustrations for this book were composed digitally.
The text was set in Berkeley Oldstyle Book, and the display type is Fontesque.

Little, Brown and Company
Hachette Book Group
1290 Avenue of the Americas, New York, NY 10104
Visit us at lb-kids.com

Little, Brown and Company is a division of Hachette Book Group, Inc.
The Little, Brown name and logo are trademarks of Hachette Book Group, Inc.

The publisher is not responsible for websites (or their content) that are not owned by the publisher.

First Edition: July 2017

Library of Congress Cataloging-in-Publication Data
Names: Colfer, Chris, 1990– author. | Dorman, Brandon, illustrator.
Title: Trollbella throws a party : a tale from the Land of Stories / by Chris Colfer ; illustrated by Brandon Dorman.
Description: First edition. | New York ; Boston : Little, Brown and Company, 2017. | Summary: Trollbella, a young queen, throws herself
the most wonderful birthday party imaginable, but does not begin to enjoy it until she hears a laugh coming from the Ferris wheel.
Identifiers: LCCN 2015040167 | ISBN 9780316383400 (hardcover)
Subjects: | CYAC: Parties—Fiction. | Birthdays—Fiction. | Kings, queens, rulers, etc.—Fiction. |
Generosity—Fiction. | Trolls—Fiction.
Classification: LCC PZ7.C677474 Tro 2016 | DDC [E]—dc23
LC record available at http://lccn.loc.gov/2015040167

ISBNs: 978-0-316-38340-0 (hardcover), 978-0-316-43542-0 (ebook),
978-0-316-43543-7 (ebook), 978-0-316-43541-3 (ebook)

10 9 8 7 6 5 4 3 2 1

APS

Printed in China